WEST LAFAYETTE PUBLIC LIBRARY
3 1951 00245 534
W9-BTS-365

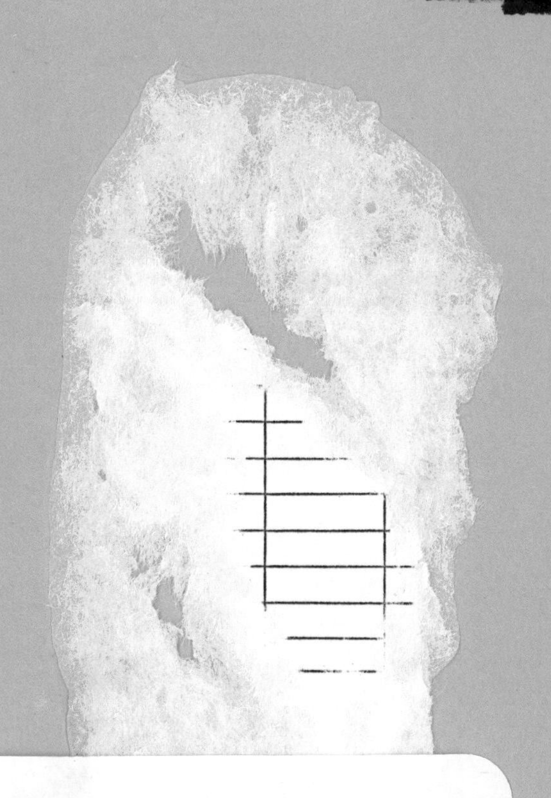

# P·E·N·N·Y

Beatrice Schenk de Regniers

# P·E·N·N·Y

illustrated by Betsy Lewin

LOTHROP, LEE & SHEPARD BOOKS
NEW YORK

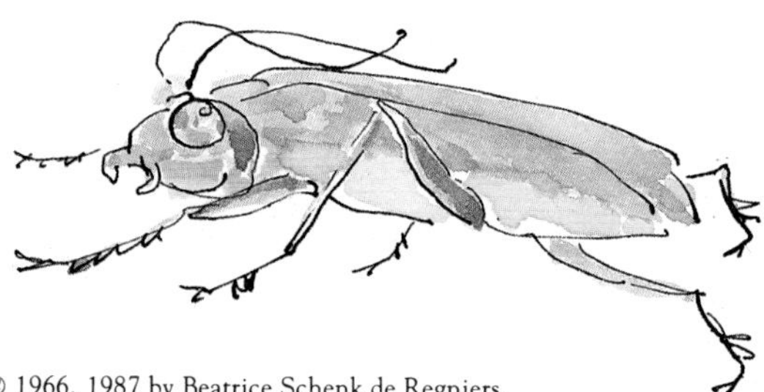

 Inquiries should be addressed to Lothrop, Lee & Shepard Books, a division of William Morrow & Company, Inc., 105 Madison Avenue, New York, New York 10016.
Printed in the United States of America.
Revised Edition

1 2 3 4 5 6 7 8 9 10

Library of Congress Cataloging in Publication Data

De Regniers, Beatrice Schenk.
Penny.
Summary: A little girl, no bigger than a penny, is adopted by an old man and an old woman who try to find a special husband for her, but she rebels and finds her own.
[1. Fairy tales. 2. Size—Fiction] I. Lewin, Betsy, ill. II. Title.
PZ8.D45Pe 1986 [E] 85-23762
ISBN 0-688-06264-4
ISBN 0-688-06265-2 (lib. bdg.)

For Lillian F. Goldman,
with love

# CONTENTS

# 1.

The old man was fishing.
It was very hot.
And it was very quiet.

No birds were singing.
No dogs were barking.
No wind was blowing.
No leaf was falling.

Then all at once—
*"Help! Help!"*
—the old man heard a tiny sound.

He heard it and he didn't hear it.
The sound was so tiny he couldn't be sure.

*"Help! Help! Please help!"*

There it was again! Who could be calling?

Was the sound coming from the river?
The old man looked.

He saw a leaf on the water.

Was the sound coming from the leaf?
The old man looked.

He saw a little girl on the leaf.

A *very* little girl. She was no bigger than a penny.

The leaf was floating down the river. And the little girl was calling, "*Help! Help!*"

The old man scooped up the leaf with the little girl on it.

"Thank you," said the little girl.

She spoke so softly, the old man could not hear what she was saying.

"WHAT?" said the old man.

"Oh!" said the little girl. "Don't speak so loud. You will blow me away!"

"I will speak more softly," said the old man. "But you must speak louder."

And he held the little girl close to his ear. . . .

## 2.

The old man came home.

"Wife," said the old man. "We have been wishing and wishing for a little girl. And now we have a little girl. A *very* little girl."

The old man put the little girl on the table.

"OH!" said the old woman.

"Don't speak so loud," said the old man. "You will blow her away."

"Oh," said the old woman softly. "What a pretty little girl. She is so *pretty*. And she is so little. She is no bigger than a penny."

Then the old woman said to the little girl, "We will call you Penny."

"Penny *is* my name," said the little girl. "What is your name?"

"Call me Aunty," said the old woman.

"Call me Uncle," said the old man.

"Aunty!" said Penny. "Uncle!" And she blew them a tiny kiss.

# 3.

*Meow,* said the cat.

"Come," said Aunty. "You must meet our family."

And she called
the cat
and the dog
and the rabbit
and the turtle
and the bird.

"This is Penny," said the old woman.

"Cat, she is not a mouse.
Do not pounce on her.

"Dog, she is not a toy. Do not chew her.

"Rabbit, she is not a flower.
Do not nibble her.

"Turtle, she is not a bug.
Do not snap at her.

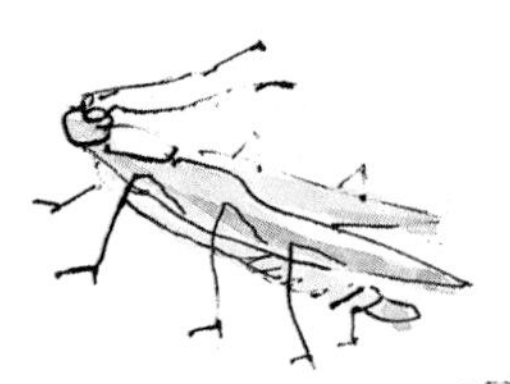

"Bird, she is not a berry. Do not eat her.

"Penny is our little girl. Take care of her.
Do you understand?"

*Meow,* said the cat.

*Woof,* said the dog.

The rabbit wiggled his ears.

The turtle blinked his eyes.

*Cheep,* said the bird.

Now they were all friends.

The turtle let Penny ride on his back. Slowly, slowly, he took her all around the room.

The rabbit let Penny sit on his head. And they went lickety-split across the meadow.

The dog stood guard over Penny.
He would not let anyone hurt her.

The cat played hide-and-seek with Penny.

And the bird? Well, the bird and Penny sang songs together.

# 4.

The old woman loved Penny. She made dresses for Penny out of a leaf, out of a flower.

A nutshell was Penny's bed. An eggshell was her bathtub.

"What shall we do for a cup?" asked Aunty.

"Here is a flower," said Penny. "This little flower will make a big cup for me."

The old woman filled the tiny flower-cup with a drop of milk.

The old man loved Penny. He made a park for her to play in.

The flower box was Penny's park.
She climbed the geranium plant.
"This is my favorite tree," Penny said.

The old man made her a tree house.

"Uncle, I wish I had a swing," said Penny. So the old man twisted thread into a strong rope, and he made a swing out of a toothpick.

The old man made a pond for her.
He made her a little sailboat, too.

"Now I will be the wind," he said. And he blew on the sails to make the boat go.

Everyone loved Penny.
And Penny loved everyone—
the old woman, the old man,
the cat, the dog,
the rabbit, the turtle,
the bird.

And so the days went by.
And the weeks went by.

Halloween came. The old man made a jack-o'-lantern out of a cranberry. And everyone wore Halloween faces.

Christmas came.
It was easy to make a tiny Christmas tree for Penny.

So the weeks went by.
And the years went by. . . .

# 5.

"Our little Penny gets older," said the old man, "but she does not get bigger."

"Our little Penny does not get bigger," said the old woman, "but she gets prettier and prettier and prettier. Soon she will be wanting to get married."

"And where, oh, where, will we find a husband for her?" said the old man. "Only a prince can be a husband for our Penny," he said.

And for Penny's sixteenth birthday he made her a tiny crown out of golden wire.

"Now you are Princess Penny," said the old man.

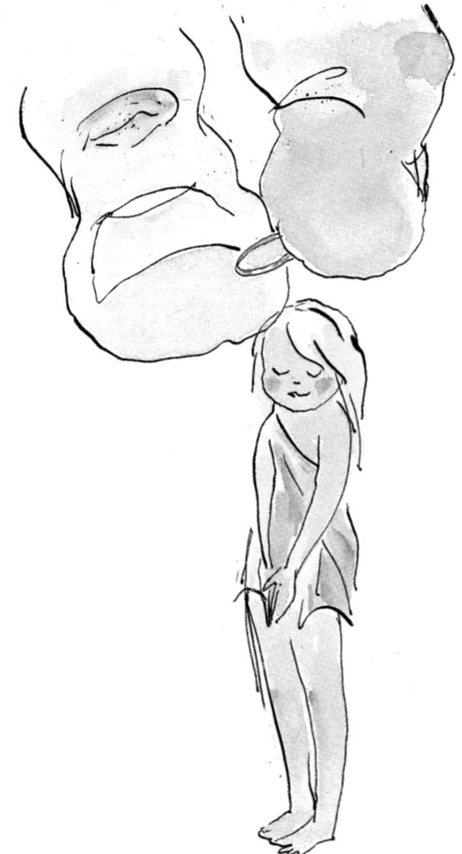

# 6.

On the morning of Penny's birthday the old man got up very early.

"I must go out and find a husband for Penny," the old man said.

"Then look for someone very little," said the old woman. "He must not be much bigger than Penny."

"He must be a prince," said the old man. "Only a prince can be a husband for our Penny."

# 7.

The old man took a very small bag with him, and he went down to the river.

A tiny green frog was sitting on the riverbank. He was no bigger than a penny.

"You are little enough," said the old man. "And you are handsome enough. Tell me, are you a frog prince? Only a prince can be a husband for our Penny."

*Peep,* said the frog.

"Then come with me," said the old man. And he put the frog into his bag.

The old man saw a tiny, furry ball. It was a field mouse, sound asleep.

The old man poked the mouse gently. "Tell me," said the old man, "are you a mouse prince?"

*Squeak,* said the mouse.

"Then come with me," said the old man. "Maybe you can be a husband for our Penny." And the old man put the tiny field mouse into his bag. The mouse went to sleep at once.

The old man walked on. And on his way he picked up a beetle. In the sunlight the beetle shone green and gold and purple.

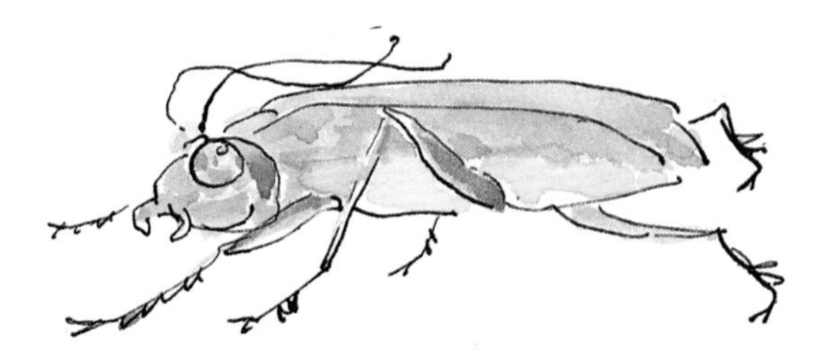

"Surely this beetle is a prince!" The old man put the beetle into his bag.

When he saw a cricket, the old man said, "If you are a cricket prince, jump into my bag." The cricket jumped into the little bag.

The old man walked on.

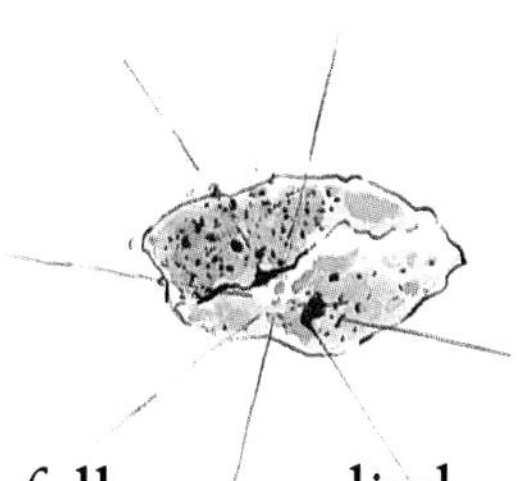

He almost fell over a little stone. He picked it up. The stone sparkled like a hundred tiny diamonds.

"Ah, surely you are the prince of stones," said the old man. "Maybe you can be a husband for our Penny."

And the old man put the little stone into his bag and went home.

# 8.

"Look, my dear," said the old man.
"I have a bag full of husbands for you.
You may choose the one you want."
And he opened the bag.

The frog hopped out.
The cricket jumped out.
The beetle crawled out of the bag.

Then the field mouse woke up and ran out of the bag. He almost knocked Penny over.

"Help!" said Penny.

"You may choose the husband you want," said the old man. "Every one of them is a prince."

*Peep,* said the frog.

Penny did not know whether to laugh or to cry.

"Uncle! Uncle!" said Penny. "Dear Uncle, how could I marry a frog or a cricket or a beetle or a mouse?"

"But every one of them is a prince!" said the old man.

"Then I do not want a prince for a husband," said Penny. There were tears in her eyes.

"Wait!" said the old man. "I have one more husband for you. Ah, how handsome!" And he turned the bag upside down.

Out fell the little stone.

"See," said the old man.
"He sparkles like a hundred diamonds.
He is the prince of stones!"

"No!" Penny said. "I will *not* have a stone for a husband. And I will not have a frog
or a cricket
or a beetle
or a mouse!"

And she stamped her foot.

"You are very hard to please," said the old man. For the first time, he spoke crossly to Penny.

Penny burst into tears and ran to hide under some violets.

"Ah!" said the old man. "I have tried and tried to please you. And this is the thanks I get. Tomorrow you must choose a husband. Do you hear me?" he shouted.

Penny did not answer.

She lay hidden under the violets, with her hands over her ears. And she was sobbing, sobbing as though her heart would break.

# 9.

In the morning Penny got up very early. She whistled softly to the bird, and he came to her at once.

Then Penny climbed on the bird's back, whispered something to him, and away they flew.

# 10.

When the old woman woke up,
she saw that Penny was gone.
The bird was gone, too.

"Penny!" she called. "Penny! Penny . . .
Penny!" And the old woman began to cry.

"Don't cry," said the old man. "Penny and the bird will come back. They will come back before the sun goes down."

But the sun went down. The moon came up. And Penny and the bird did not come back.

The next day was Monday. All day Monday they waited, and all day Tuesday.

But Penny and the bird did not come back.

# 11.

Where was Penny?
Where had she gone with the bird?

Penny was looking for her country—the country of the tiny people.

"I remember that my country is near a river," Penny said to the bird. "It is where

a river begins. That is all I can remember.
So we must fly this way."

They flew all that day.
And they flew all night.

The next day it rained. Penny and the bird stayed under a bush all day. Penny sat close to the bird, under his wing.

That night the rain stopped. The moon came out. And so did the stars.

Penny climbed on the bird's back and they flew all night long.

When morning came, the bird was tired. Penny was hungry.

The bird flew down to the riverbank to rest, and Penny looked for wild berries.

All at once, Penny heard a lovely sound.

Was someone singing? The sound was so far away, she couldn't be sure.

Now the sound came closer. Yes, someone was singing. . . .

# 12.

Penny heard a tiny voice singing—
*"Oh, I'm looking for a teeny-tiny wife-wife-wife. . . ."*

Who could be singing?

*"When I find her, I will keep her all my life-life-life!"*

Was the sound coming from the river?
Penny looked.

A leaf was floating on the water.

A young man was standing on the leaf.
He was steering it with a twig.

The young man was not much bigger than
Penny, and he was singing—
"*Oh, any wife of miney must be
very teeny-tiny. And if she is
brave and kind and smart . . . she
will surely, surely win my heart. . . .*"

Penny leaned far over the water and waved her handkerchief. "*Help! Help!*" she called.

The young man saw her at once, and he steered his leaf toward the shore.

"My name is Nicolas," he said, "and I want to marry you. I can see that you are brave. I think you must be kind. You are probably smart, too."

"Thank you," said Penny. "Can you take me to the country of the tiny people?"

"Alas, no," said Nicolas. "The country of the tiny people is far, far up the river. My leaf-boat can only go *down* the river."

"My bird can take us there if you will show him the way," said Penny. She held out her hand, and Nicolas jumped onto the riverbank. Penny whistled softly, and the bird came to her at once.

"There is someplace we must go first," Penny told Nicolas. "I must say goodbye to Uncle and Aunty."

# 13.

As soon as Penny and Nicolas climbed on his back, the bird began to fly home.

He flew all day and he flew all night.

Then on Wednesday morning, the bird was home again. And Penny and Nicolas were with him.

"Aunty," said Penny, "this is Nicolas.
He wants to marry me."

Nicolas stood up very straight.
Oh! He looked wise, and strong,
and handsome!

He bowed to the old woman. He bowed to the old man.

"I want to marry Penny," said Nicolas.

"I want to marry Nicolas," said Penny.

"We want Penny to be happy," said the old woman.

"We are glad Penny has found a husband," said the old man. He forgot to ask if Nicolas was a prince.

# 14.

So the old woman made a big
wedding cake. And Penny made
her own wedding dress.

Nicolas and Penny stood on top of the
wedding cake.

It was a beautiful wedding.

# 15.

Penny and Nicolas got ready to fly away on their wedding trip.

"When will you come back?" asked the old woman.

"We will build you a little house in the flower box," said the old man.

"No. No, thank you," said Nicolas. "Penny must come with me to our country of the tiny people. That is where we will make our home."

"No! No! Penny!" the old woman cried. "How can you leave us? How can we live without you?"

Penny looked at Nicolas. Then she looked at the old woman, and she looked at the old man.

The old woman was sobbing.
The old man was crying.

"Aunty, Uncle," said Penny softly, "I must leave you. But I will come back. We will come to see you every year when it is Halloween."

"And we will come again at Christmas," Nicolas said.

The old woman was not sobbing now.

"And when it is Valentine's Day,
we will come to bring you a valentine,"
Penny said.

"We will come on your birthdays to wish you happy birthday," said Nicolas.

The old man wiped the tears off his mustache.

"Yes," said Penny. "And then it will be Halloween again!"

Now everyone began to laugh.

So the old woman and the old man kissed Penny and Nicolas goodbye . . .

and the bird flew away with Penny and Nicolas toward the country of the tiny people.

Beatrice Schenk de Regniers has written such marvelous books for children as *Red Riding Hood Retold in Verse,* illustrated by Edward Gorey, *Little Sister and the Month Brothers,* illustrated by Margot Tomes, and the classic *May I Bring a Friend?,* illustrated by Beni Montresor, which won the Caldecott Medal. *Penny,* first published in 1966, is one of her favorite stories.

She lives in New York City.

Betsy Lewin lives in Brooklyn, New York, with her husband Ted and their two cats, Dundee and Bones. Her drawings for Berniece Freschet's *Furlie Cat* were praised as "marvels of feline expression" by *The Horn Book Magazine* and as "robust pictures sure to please" by *Kirkus Reviews.*

"You can't fool me," Flora said. She saw the hungry look in the eagle's eye. "He's my brother and I'm taking him home."

"If the wind lets you," said the eagle.

Flora and Crispin flew on and on until they came upon the man in the moon.

"Will you give me that little boy?" asked the man in the moon. "It's lonely up here, and he could keep me company."

The man in the moon had a kind face, and he did look awfully lonely. But there were no chocolate chip cookies on the moon, and Crispin was so fond of chocolate chip cookies. "I'm sorry, but I can't," said Flora. "He's my brother and I'm taking him home."

"If the wind lets you," said the man in the moon.

Flora stomped her foot—or would have if there'd been anything to stomp on. "I'm tired of hearing that. Why won't the wind let us go home?"

"You should ask him," answered the man in the moon.

Flora hadn't thought of that. "Oh, wind, will you let us go home?"

"I'll let *you* go home as soon as we find the right spot for Crispin," replied the wind. "You do want to get rid of him, right?"

"Yes. I mean, I did. I mean—" Flora wasn't sure what she meant.

"Because I could even use him myself," said the wind. "You know, to work my bellows."

“No, thank you.” Flora had finally decided. “I should take him home. My mother wouldn’t like it if I lost him.”

“If that’s what you really want,” said the wind.

“Yes, please,” said Flora.

So the wind turned Flora and Crispin around and blew them home.

Flora put her super-special heavy-duty red boots back on, then straightened Crispin's hat and brushed a shred of rainbow from his coat.

She rang the doorbell and her mother opened the door.

"I decided to bring Crispin back," Flora told her.

"From where?" asked her mother.

"From the moon," said Flora.

"Nonsense," said her mother. "Now come inside. I've made chocolate chip cookies."